I wish

m

Zuzu's Wishing Cake

Written by Linda Michelin

Illustrated by D. B. Johnson

Houghton Mifflin Company Boston 2006

www.houghtonmifflinbooks.com

The text of this book is set in Futura.
The illustrations are mixed media.

Library of Congress Cataloging-in-Publication Data
Michelin, Linda.
Zuzu's wishing cake / written by Linda Michelin; illustrated by
D. B. Johnson.
p. cm.
Summary: When Zuzu smiles at the new boy next door
and he does not smile back, she makes him a series of gifts
that she thinks he needs.

ISBN 0-618-64640-X (hardcover)

[1. Neighborliness—Fiction. 2. Friendship—Fiction.
3. Handicraft—Fiction. 4. Moving, Household—Fiction.]
I. Johnson, D. B. (Donald B.), 1944– ill. II. Title.
PZ7.J6325238Zuz 2006
[E]—dc22
2005025442

ISBN-13: 978-0618-64640-1

Printed in China
Leo 10 9 8 7 6 5 4 3 2 1

For
Alice and Rolland Michelin

Zuzu smiles a lot.

Zuzu smiles at bags,

and boots,

and bottle caps.

She smiles at
big boxes.

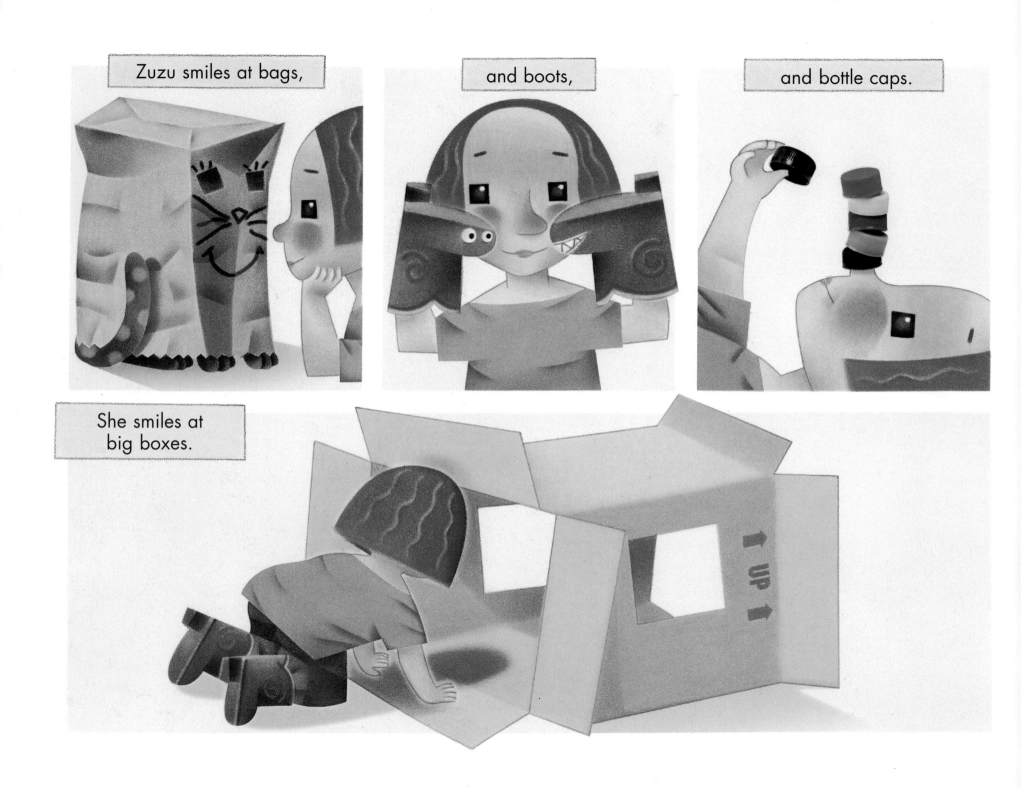

Zuzu smiles at the new boy next door.

But he does not smile back.

He just sits inside.

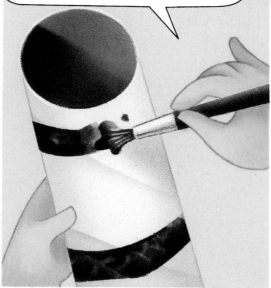

Zuzu drives to
the new boy's house.

She puts the telescope on his windowsill.

Zuzu drives
away fast.

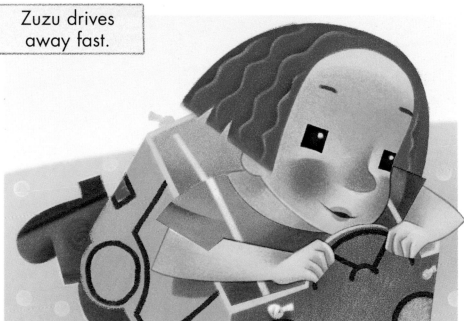

The new boy does not come outside.

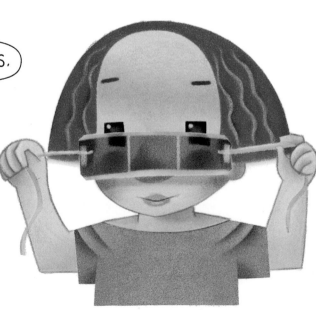

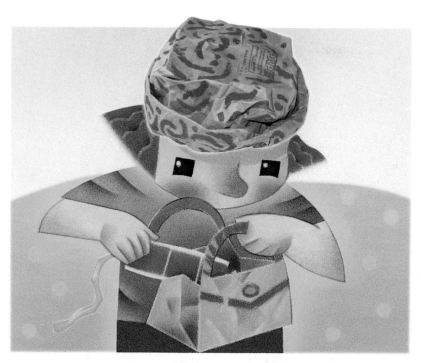

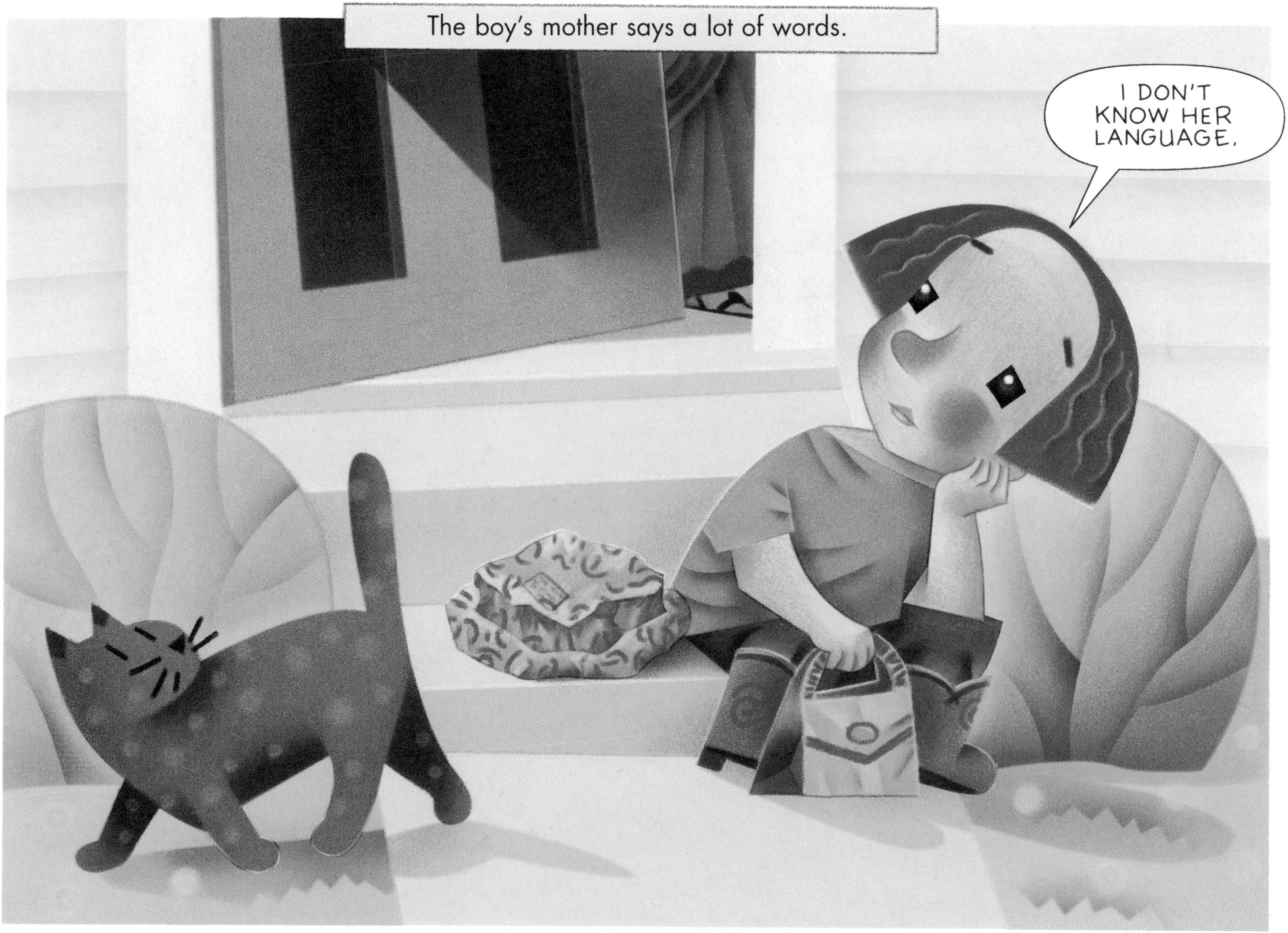
The boy's mother says a lot of words.
I DON'T KNOW HER LANGUAGE.

Still, the new boy does not come outside.

Zuzu thinks.

The stars sparkle.

I LOVE WISHING.

DOES THE NEW BOY KNOW ABOUT WISHING CAKES?

YOU CAN HAVE A WISHING CAKE ANYTIME.
NOT JUST ON YOUR BIRTHDAY.
FIRST YOU TAKE OUT SOME LAYERS.
THEN YOU CUT OFF THE SIDES.

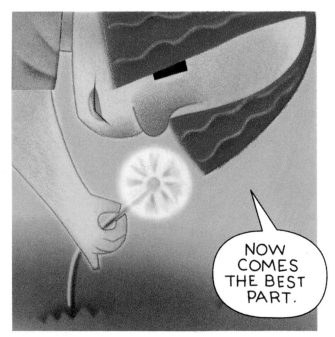

It tickles Zuzu's nose.

Hashim smiles a lot.

JUST LIKE ZUZU!